GO WEST, AMELIA BEDELIA!

BY HERMAN PARISH

PICTURES BY LYNN SWEAT

Greenwillow Books, *An Imprint of* HarperCollins*Publishers*

Library of Congress Cataloging-in-Publication Data

Parish, Herman.
Go west, Amelia Bedelia! / by Herman Parish ; illustrated by Lynn Sweat.
p. cm.
"Greenwillow Books."
Summary: Amelia Bedelia, the literal-minded housekeeper, takes a vacation at
her Uncle Buck's dude ranch.
ISBN 978-0-06-084361-8 (trade bdg.) — ISBN 978-0-06-084362-5 (lib. bdg.)
[1. Dude ranches—Fiction. 2. Ranch life—Fiction. 3. Uncles—Fiction. 4. Humorous stories.]
I. Sweat, Lynn, ill. II. Title.
PZ7.P2185Gn 2011   [E]—dc22   2010012429

10 11 12 13 14 SCP 10 9 8 7 6 5 4 3 2 1
First Edition

 Greenwillow Books

For Johnie & Julie,
Bill & Patty,
and all my Wyoming friends
—H. P.

To Elynor
—L. S.

Out West, they still talk about the day

the stranger came to town . . .

"Good morning, Uncle Buck,"

said Amelia Bedelia.

"Top of the morning to you, Amelia Bedelia,"

said Buck Bedelia, as he tipped his hat.

"You look like a rootin' tootin' cowgirl."

"Thanks to you," said Amelia Bedelia.

"This outfit you loaned me is perfect.

When it was time for my vacation,

I wanted to go on an adventure.

So, I came out West to visit you."

"I'm glad you did," said Uncle Buck.

"When I started my dude ranch,

I invited my relatives to visit anytime.

Welcome to the Double B Ranch."

A tall cowboy stepped forward.

"Howdy, ma'am," he said.

"I'm Jake, the ranch foreman."

"You're the four man?" said Amelia Bedelia.

"Where are the one, two, and three men?"

"You can meet them later," said Buck.

"Jake will teach you how to ride."

"I have never been on a horse before,"

  said Amelia Bedelia.

"You need a gentle one," said Buck.

"Jake, which horse did you pick out for her?"

  Jake smiled, winked at Buck, then said,

"I can't decide between Tornado or Dynamite."

Buck smiled back and said,

"I'll decide. Put a saddle on Cream Puff."

"Oh goody," said Amelia Bedelia.

"That is one of my favorite desserts."

"You'll love this Cream Puff," said Buck.

"She is sweet and completely broken."

"Who broke her?" said Amelia Bedelia.

"Can she be fixed so I can ride her?"

"Cream Puff is fine," said Jake.

"She was broken in for gentle riding.
It's like when you break in
a new pair of boots—
they feel better."

"Speaking of shoes," said Uncle Buck,

"meet Smitty, our expert blacksmith.

Smitty shoes all our horses."

A burly cowboy stepped forward.

"Hey there," said Smitty.

"Would you like to shoe a horse?"

"I already know how," said Amelia Bedelia.

"I can show you right now."

"Shoo!" hollered Amelia Bedelia.

She waved her bonnet all around.

"Shoo, you horsies—SHOO!"

The horses in the corral scattered.

Buck whispered to Smitty,

"I don't think Amelia Bedelia

has got much horse sense."

Smitty shook his head and said,

"Beg your pardon, boss,

but does she have any sense at all?"

Buck shook his head and sighed.

"I hope she is better at riding horses

than she is at shoeing them."

A ranch hand led over

a beautiful, cream-colored horse.

"You must be Cream Puff,"

said Amelia Bedelia.

"We will be good friends."

The horse nickered and nuzzled her.

NEIGHHH!

"I can't wait to ride!" said Amelia Bedelia.

"Do I jump on, climb on, hop on . . . ?"

"Whoa," said Jake. "Hold your horses!"

Amelia Bedelia threw her arms

around Cream Puff's neck.

Jake took things step by step.

"First," he said, "let go of your horse.

Then take hold of the saddle horn."

"Will it honk?" asked Amelia Bedelia.

"Saddle horns are silent," said Jake.

"This is a horse, not a car."

Amelia Bedelia grabbed the saddle horn.

"Now," said Jake, "put your foot

right in the stirrup, pull yourself up,

then swing your other leg over."

Amelia Bedelia put her right foot in the stirrup,

pulled herself up,

swung her leg over . . .

and sat in the saddle.

"I'm going backward," said Amelia Bedelia.

Jake could not believe his eyes.

He said, "You're getting off on the wrong foot."

"Actually," said Amelia Bedelia,

"I got on on the right foot.

Right must be wrong."

"You are starting to confuse me," said Jake.

Amelia Bedelia got down and tried again.

This time she stepped up with her left foot,

swung her leg over,

and sat tall in the saddle.

Then Jake mounted his horse, too.

"What's your horse's name?" she asked.

"Two Bits," said Jake. "He's a quarter horse."

"You got a good deal," said Amelia Bedelia.

"That horse is worth at least a dollar."

Amelia Bedelia and Jake

rode up into the mountains,

down into the valleys,

and across streams and creeks.

They came to a ghost town.

"See that place?" said Jake.

"Buck's great-great-grandfather

was the sheriff there."

"That's amazing," said Amelia Bedelia.

"Yup," said Jake. "He was a legend.

One time, an outlaw rode into town.

He had a big price on his head.

He was going to paint the town red

and then fix Sheriff Bedelia's wagon."

"He sounds very handy," said Amelia Bedelia.

"Only at making trouble," said Jake.

"Sheriff Bedelia tossed him in the cooler."

"How nice," said Amelia Bedelia.

"That might feel good

on a hot day like today."

25

When Jake and Amelia Bedelia returned,

Uncle Buck was there to greet them.

He helped Amelia Bedelia off her horse.

Her first steps were pretty wobbly.

"Attagirl!" said Uncle Buck. "You survived.

How's my favorite tenderfoot?"

"Most of me is fine," said Amelia Bedelia.

"My feet are not the part that is tender."

Uncle Buck chuckled.

"You are just saddle sore," he said.

"Rub this liniment on whatever hurts.

 I use it on my horse and on myself.

 It will cure man or beast."

"Gosh," said Amelia Bedelia,

"I am neither one of those,

 but I'll try anything that might help."

The next morning, all the ranch guests

met down at the corral for a lesson.

"Hi, I'm Carol," said a cowgirl.

"I'll teach you how to lasso a steer."

Carol showed them how to twirl a lariat

around and around over their heads,

then let it go at just the right time.

"It's easy," said Carol. "Who wants to try?"

Amelia Bedelia stepped right up.

She twirled the lariat around, then let go,

but her bonnet got in the way.

Uncle Buck wandered by.

"Keeping busy?" he asked.

"I'm trying," said Amelia Bedelia.

"Right now I'm a little tied up."

"So I see," said Uncle Buck.

"Sometimes it's good to know

how the cow feels."

Uncle Buck untangled her.

Then he showed Amelia Bedelia

how to lasso a steer instead of herself.

He threw in some rope tricks for fun.

"You know," said Uncle Buck.

"Cowboys lead a tough life.

We punch cows and wrestle steers."

"You do?" said Amelia Bedelia.

"That sounds tougher on the cows."

"We take care of them, too," said Uncle Buck.

"In a few days, we'll drive all the cattle

to greener pastures with fresh grass to eat."

"You drive every cow?" said Amelia Bedelia.

"Each and every one," said Uncle Buck.

Amelia Bedelia was excited.

She turned to go practice her lassoing.

"Yikes!" yelled Amelia Bedelia.

"That bush wasn't there a minute ago."

"That's a tumbleweed," said Uncle Buck.

"It is supposed to tumble, not you."

He helped her up and brushed her off.

"Ouch!" said Amelia Bedelia.

"It's time for some more liniment."

The wind blew the tumbleweed on its way.

Amelia Bedelia worked hard

to get ready for the cattle drive.

She rode Cream Puff twice a day.

She got better with a lasso.

She even practiced rope tricks.

On the day of the cattle drive,

Amelia Bedelia woke up bright and early.

"Morning," said Uncle Buck.

"You look happier every day.

Do you feel at home on the range?"

"Absolutely," said Amelia Bedelia.

"I can cook on any range, gas or electric."

Uncle Buck chuckled and said,

"Would you help our cook make lunch?

He's stocking up the chuck wagon."

"Sure!" said Amelia Bedelia.

"May I help you, Chuck?"

asked Amelia Bedelia.

"Much obliged," said the cook.

"Just don't call me Chuck."

"I'm sorry," said Amelia Bedelia.

"Would you prefer Charles?"

"No," he said. "My name is Andy."

"So where is Chuck?" said Amelia Bedelia.

"Did you borrow Chuck's wagon?"

"'Chuck' is what cowboys call food," Andy explained.

" This chuck wagon is a rolling kitchen.

I'm heading out to cook for the cattle drive."

"I'll give you a hand," said Amelia Bedelia.

Andy took her hand

and pulled her up on the wagon.

"Giddyup!" he called to the mule.

The Double B chuck wagon lurched forward.

After about an hour on the trail,

Amelia Bedelia asked, "What's for lunch?"

"Well," said Andy, "today it's chili."

Amelia Bedelia looked at the burning sun.

"Chilly?" she said. "It's going to be hot."

"You bet," said Andy. "I love hot chili."

Amelia Bedelia felt very confused.

"In that case," she said,

"what's for dessert—cold warm?"

"Huh?" said Andy, yawning.

He handed the reins to Amelia Bedelia.

"I'm tired," he said. "You drive for a bit."

"Where do I go?" asked Amelia Bedelia.

"Just follow the trail," said Andy.

"Then turn left at the creek."

A minute later, Andy was snoozing.

Amelia Bedelia enjoyed driving.

As she passed a prairie dog village,

she heard a loud creak.

The breeze was blowing

a rusty gate back and forth.

CREAK, CUH-REAK! CRREEEEAAK!!

"There's the creak," said Amelia Bedelia.

She turned the wagon to the left.

Amelia Bedelia drove a while longer.

Then she heard a much louder noise.

The noise got so loud, it woke up Andy.

"What's that racket?" he asked. "Where are we?"

"I turned left at the creak," said Amelia Bedelia.

"Should I turn right at the rumble?"

Andy looked like he had seen a ghost.

"Stampede!" he hollered.

He grabbed the reins and shouted, "Hee-yah!"

The rumble grew louder and louder.

A herd of cattle was headed straight for them.

Amelia Bedelia waved her bonnet and shouted,

"SHOO! Shoo, you cows! Shoo, I say!"

The cattle stopped dead in their tracks.

They stared straight at Amelia Bedelia.

They had never seen anything like her.

Just then, Uncle Buck and the others rode up.

"Amelia Bedelia!" he said. "Are you okay?

The herd got spooked by a noise,

but you stopped the stampede single-handed!"

"No," said Amelia Bedelia. "I used both hands.

And Andy deserves as much credit as I do."

All the other cowboys cheered and whistled.

"I say it's time for lunch," said Andy.

"Come and get it!" yelled Amelia Bedelia.

Hungry cowboys surrounded the chuck wagon.

"I'm famous for my three-bean chili," said Andy.

"These guys are starved," said Amelia Bedelia.

"You'd better serve them more than three beans."

Andy handed her the first bowl of his chili.

"Wow!" said Amelia Bedelia. "This is spicy.

I could eat this hot, warm, cold, or chilly."

After lunch, Carol played a guitar.

The cowboys sang their favorite songs.

Amelia Bedelia joined in on the chorus:

"Come-a-tie-yie-yippy-yippy-yay-yippy-yay!"

They sang songs all the way back to the ranch.

The next morning, it was time

for Amelia Bedelia to go back home.

Everyone gathered to say good-bye.

Carol gave Amelia Bedelia a lariat.

Smitty gave her a horseshoe for luck.

Andy gave her his three-bean chili recipe.

Even Cream Puff came to say good-bye.

"Are you my present?" said Amelia Bedelia.

Jake said, "You know what they say:

Don't look a gift horse in the mouth."

"That's good advice," said Amelia Bedelia.

"It might have bad breath."

Jake gave her more liniment.

They both laughed.

"I got you new duds," said Uncle Buck.

"Duds?" said Amelia Bedelia.

"If they don't work, why get new ones?"

"'Duds' is cowboy talk," said Uncle Buck.

"That's what we call clothes."

"This hat is huge!" said Amelia Bedelia.

"It's a ten-gallon hat," said Uncle Buck.

"Wow," said Amelia Bedelia.

"With ten gallons, I'll never go thirsty."

Amelia Bedelia hugged Uncle Buck.

"Thank you so much," she said.

"You gave me such wonderful memories."

"My pleasure," said Uncle Buck.

"You are a legend for stopping that stampede.

Folks will never forget you or your bonnet."

Amelia Bedelia handed him her bonnet.

"Here is my present to you," she said.

"Keep it handy in case of another stampede."

"I sure will," said Uncle Buck.

"I will keep it in a place of honor."

"Thanks again for these duds,"

said Amelia Bedelia.

"I'll get changed and go home in style."

As Amelia Bedelia rode away,

Uncle Buck called out, "Come back anytime,

and bring Cousin Alcolu with you."

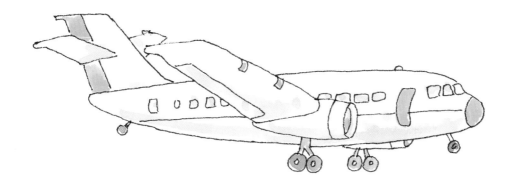

Back East, they still talk about the day

Amelia Bedelia came home from vacation.

"Howdy," said Amelia Bedelia.

"Amelia Bedelia?" said Mrs. Rogers.

"Is that really you?"

"Yup," said Amelia Bedelia.

"You bet your boots, pardners."

"In that case," said Mr. Rogers,

"Let's mosey on back to the bunkhouse,

and you can rustle up some grub for us."

"Now you're talking," said Amelia Bedelia.

"Come and get it!" said Amelia Bedelia.

At dinner, Amelia Bedelia told Mr. and Mrs. Rogers

all about her adventures out West.

And she used more than three beans in the chili.